P9-EMO-812

FATIMA'S GREAT OUTDOORS

by ambreen tariq   illustrated by stevie lewis

Anderson County Library
Anderson, S.C.
ACL-IVA

Kokila

Fatima and her aapa stood at the curb and waited for their parents to pick them up from school. Today, they weren't going straight home. Today, the Khazi family was going camping for the first time. Camping, her father had told them over dinner in his teaching voice, was a great American pastime.

The trip felt like Fatima's reward after a long, hard week.

On Monday, some kids wrinkled their noses at her lunch;

on Tuesday, someone in class laughed and told her it's pronounced "fractions," not "furrrrrrrrr-actions";

on Wednesday, a boy
pulled on her long braid
in the hallway;

and on Thursday,
she didn't do so well
on her math quiz.

Fatima smiled when her parents pulled up. The sisters piled into the car, squeezing in between pillows, blankets, and a big cardboard box filled with cooking supplies. "Wow, this is a lot of stuff!" Fatima yelled. "Are we moving to the forest?"

Mama asked the girls in Urdu if they were excited as she reached back to hand them warm homemade samosas. The girls nodded vigorously with jack-o'-lantern smiles. Mama's samosas always tasted extra delicious on road trips. "How about some gaane?" Papa asked. Mohammed Rafi's voice rose from the car speakers and Bollywood songs spilled out from the windows. Fatima's cares melted away as they all sang along in Hindi.

Aapa shouted over the music and announced to the whole car how well she had done on her math homework. Aapa's teacher even asked her to come to the front of the class and solve a hard problem on the board that most of the other kids had gotten wrong. "Shabash!" Papa said with pride.

Aapa went on and on about school. Fatima slumped in her seat and ate another samosa.

As Fatima thought about how to change the topic, her big sister pointed out the window and shouted: "Look! We're here!" The family cheered as they passed the sign for the state park.

At the campsite, the girls helped their parents unload.

"First," Papa said, "we must build our tent."

Aapa and Mama chose to start dinner instead. Fatima watched as Papa took the tent gear out of a sack.

Papa grumbled in Urdu when the pieces wouldn't fit. Fatima wanted to help, but could she?
She hadn't done anything right at school that week—what would make the campground
any different?

Fatima took a tiny step closer.

She suggested to Papa that they read the
instruction manual together.

When they finished, Fatima stood proudly next to their brand-new home in the forest. "Shabash!" Papa's bear paw clapped her shoulder.

The Khazi family celebrated the start of their first camping trip over a delicious dinner of shami kabab and rotis that Mama had brought from home.

After dinner, Fatima and Aapa crawled into the family tent. They were so excited to snooze in their new sleeping bags. They never had rooms of their own, not even in India, so being together in one big tent felt cozy and right. The girls zipped up their sleeping bags and chattered on as their parents finished cleaning up.

Aapa was telling Fatima about how she won her class spelling bee when suddenly her face dropped. She gasped and pointed to the tent ceiling. Eight long, giant legs gripped the outside of their tent.

"A monster!" The girls screamed and huddled together.

They cried out for Mama—she was fearless and would know what to do. When they lived in India, Mama would catch the lizards and throw them out without flinching. That's why she had that funny finger, Aapa said. She had been getting rid of a scorpion from her house when it stung her.

The monster moved across the roof and the girls screamed again. "What's going on?!" Mama shouted over the sound of dishes being washed. The Khazis didn't use paper plates because they were too expensive.

"Mama, don't open the tent," Aapa yelled. "There's a giant, poisonous spider monster outside!"

"Don't be silly, it's tiny," Mama replied impatiently. "Go brush your teeth before bed."

Mama held the tent door flaps and on the count of three, the girls ran out. They followed the same precautions coming back inside: 1, 2, 3 . . . they zoomed into their sleeping bags in a single, fluid motion.

That night, Fatima had a hard time falling asleep. Crickets chirped and wind blew against their tent. She flinched every time a twig snapped. But soon, as the trees swayed outside, Fatima's eyes got heavy and she drifted into a warm, deep sleep that only campers enjoy. Soft snores drifted outside the Khazis' tent and joined the sounds of the forest.

The next morning, Fatima woke up to the smell of anda and roti cooking in ghee. Papa was waiting for her to make the bacon over a roaring fire. He had promised Fatima they could have bacon for breakfast just like the other American families. They had even made a special trip to the Halal butcher shop for the beef kind. "Baaher aajao!" Papa called for them to come outside. The sisters crept out slowly.

Mama pointed at the top of the tent between chuckles. "Go look at your big monster," she said. A harmless little daddy longlegs sat quietly between beads of morning dew. It had been guarding them from mosquitos all night. The girls laughed and laughed. Mama and Papa laughed too. Fatima was pretty sure the spider joined in as well.

"Let's start the campfire so we can make this smoky bacon you've been so excited about, Fatima!" Papa said.

Twenty minutes later, there still was no campfire. Papa grumbled under his breath in Urdu. The fire wouldn't catch.

Fatima looked around at the other families' campsites and they all had roaring fires. Why couldn't theirs look like that? Why did Fatima's family always have to be so different? She pouted and kicked rocks.

Papa kept spraying lighter fluid on the logs. The fire would scream for a second and then it would be gone. Mama came over to see what all the fuss was about. She shook her head and clicked her teeth in disapproval, the way Fatima's aunties did.

"That's not how you start a fire; let me show you," she said. "A fire, like strength, takes patience to build."

She made the girls gather twigs and dry leaves for kindling, then bigger sticks for tinder.

Unlike Papa, who grew up in big cities in India, Mama came from a small town where they had to use a woodburning stove outside to make chai when they ran out of gas for the inside stove. Fatima remembered visiting her nani's house and helping one morning. Mama showed Fatima how to use a long metal pipe to breathe oxygen into the fire; that's how it comes alive, she had said.

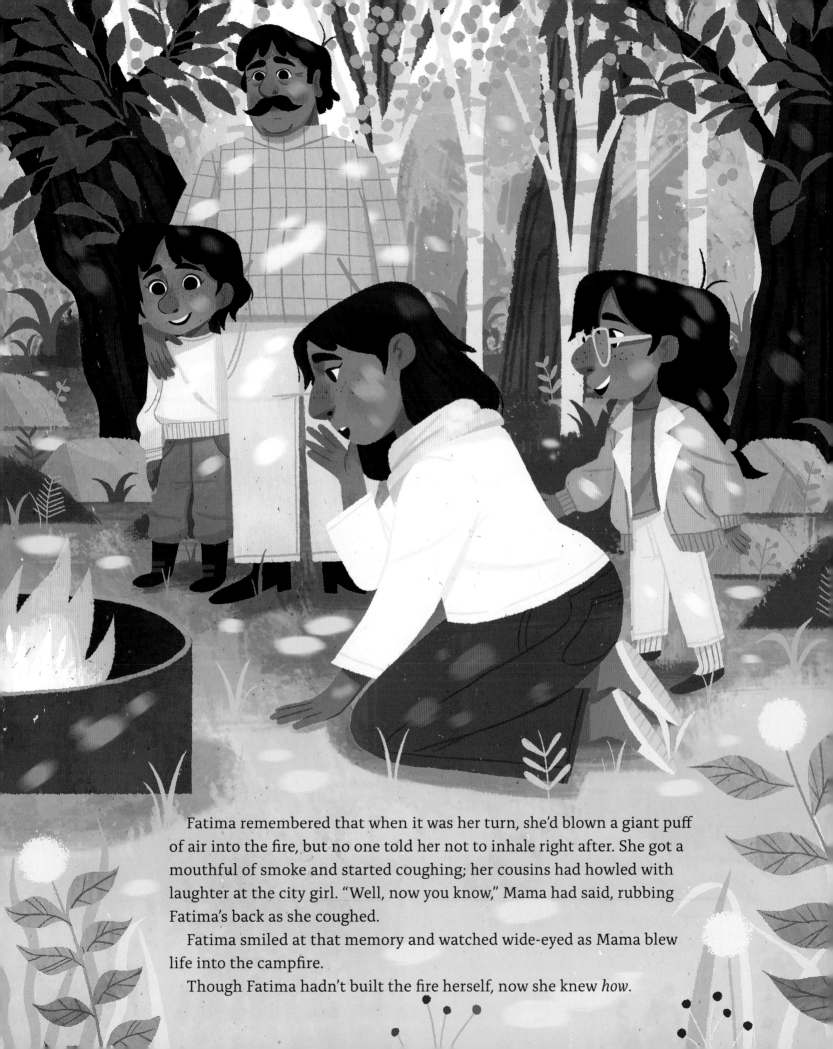

Fatima remembered that when it was her turn, she'd blown a giant puff of air into the fire, but no one told her not to inhale right after. She got a mouthful of smoke and started coughing; her cousins had howled with laughter at the city girl. "Well, now you know," Mama had said, rubbing Fatima's back as she coughed.

Fatima smiled at that memory and watched wide-eyed as Mama blew life into the campfire.

Though Fatima hadn't built the fire herself, now she knew *how*.

As the Khazi family packed up, Fatima's heart felt heavy. "I am so sad," she told Aapa. "I don't want to go home."

Home meant no laughing around the campfire or telling funny stories from India.

Home meant no long road trips with fresh samosas and Bollywood sing-alongs in the car. Home meant taking tests, doing homework, getting in trouble, and being teased at school. Home meant Mama and Papa would be tired again from working long hours and two jobs each.

Fatima looked at the tall trees and the big blue sky and the imprints in the dirt where their tent used to stand. Being outdoors reminded her of how she used to feel in India: She had fun, she didn't feel sad or scared, and she loved how adventure was around every corner. At the campground, Fatima felt like a superhero. But now, she had to leave it all behind.

Aapa rubbed Fatima's back and said, "Don't worry, we'll be back soon.
Remember, you can share all this at show-and-tell."

Fatima returned to school with stories of her Great Outdoors.
"Guess what?" she asked her classmates. "I am a superhero! I have lots of superpowers:
I can build fires and tents and I'm not afraid of spider monsters!"

Fatima beamed as she thought about what
the Khazi family's next camping adventure would hold.

To my family and to all the
little adventurers out there.
Just keep going!
—A.T.

To my friend, Yezi, for introducing
me to the outdoors.
—S.L.

KOKILA
An imprint of Penguin Random House LLC, New York

First published in the United States of America by Kokila,
an imprint of Penguin Random House LLC, 2021

Text copyright © 2021 by Ambreen Tariq
Illustrations copyright © 2021 by Stevie Danielle Lewis

Penguin supports copyright. Copyright fuels creativity, encourages diverse voices, promotes free
speech, and creates a vibrant culture. Thank you for buying an authorized edition of this book
and for complying with copyright laws by not reproducing, scanning, or distributing any part of
it in any form without permission. You are supporting writers and allowing Penguin to continue
to publish books for every reader.

Kokila & colophon are registered trademarks of Penguin Random House LLC.

Visit us online at penguinrandomhouse.com.

Library of Congress Cataloging-in-Publication Data is available.

Manufactured in China
ISBN 9781984816955

1 3 5 7 9 10 8 6 4 2

Design by Jasmin Rubero
Text set in Alda OT family

The art for this book was created digitally.

The publisher does not have any control over and does not
assume any responsibility for author or third-party websites or their content.